SHAWN and KEEPER

Show-and-Tell

by Jonathan London
illustrated by Renée Williams-Andriani

Dutton Children's Books • New York

For Sean and Keeper, and Xavier too—J.L.

To Maggie, Ellen, and Joseph—R.W.-A.

Text copyright © 2000 by Jonathan London
Illustrations copyright © 2000 by Renée Williams-Andriani

All rights reserved.

CIP Data is available.

Published in the United States 2000 by Dutton Children's Books,
a division of Penguin Putnam Books for Young Readers
345 Hudson Street, New York, New York 10014

Printed in Hong Kong

First Edition

ISBN 0-525-46114-0

3 5 7 9 10 8 6 4 2

Shawn and Keeper

did everything together.

They were the best of friends.

They walked together

and talked together.

They growled together
and howled together.

They ate together

and cleaned the plate together.

One day, Shawn said,

"Mom, I want to take Keeper

to show-and-tell on Friday!

We'll do tricks together."

"Good idea," said Mom.

On Monday, Shawn trained
Keeper to sit.

"Good boy!" Shawn said.

He gave Keeper a cookie.

On Tuesday, Shawn trained
Keeper to lie down.

"Good boy!" Shawn said.

He gave Keeper a cookie.

On Wednesday and Thursday,

Shawn trained Keeper

to shake hands and fetch.

"Good boy!" Shawn said.

He gave Keeper a cookie.

"Oh, I love you so much!" said Shawn.

"Woof!" barked Keeper.

Finally, it was Friday.

It was time for show-and-tell!

First, Leah sang to her mouse.

Then Max showed his

pet snake.

And Emma did a hat trick

with her rabbit.

"And now," said the teacher,

"Shawn's dog, Keeper,

will do some tricks!"

"Sit!" said Shawn.

But Keeper stood up.

He wagged his tail.

He licked Shawn's face.

"Lie down!" said Shawn.

But Keeper scratched his ear.

He sniffed the air.

He sniffed the teacher.

"Shake hands!" said Shawn.

But Keeper lay down

and rolled over.

All the kids scratched his belly.

"Fetch!" said Shawn.

But Keeper tripped the teacher.

He jumped over a desk.

He spilled cups of pencils

and bottles of glue.

He sent papers flying . . .

and knocked over the fish tank—

splash!

"Oh no!" cried Shawn.

When Shawn caught Keeper,

he said, "Bad boy!

But I still love you."

And he gave Keeper a cookie.

After school,

Shawn and Keeper walked together

and talked together.

They growled together

and howled together.

They were the best of friends.